The Truth (and Myths) About
Thanksgiving

by L. A. Peacock

Illustrated by Nick Wigsby

Scholastic Inc.

For Shelly, Lucille, Wayne, and Steve —
my Greenhouse lunch buddies. –L.A.F.

Thank you to the following for their kind permission
to use their photographs in this book:

Photographs © 2013: AP Images/North Wind Picture Archives: 38;
Corbis Images/Roman Soumar: 33; Courtesy of Plimoth Plantation:
43, 57; Shutterstock, Inc./Mike Loiselle: 54; Superstock, Inc./Jean Leon
Gerome Ferris: 19; The Granger Collection: 50 (Charles W. Jefferys), 61
(Felix O.C. Darley), 13 (Marshall Johnson).

ISBN 978-0-545-56846-3

12 11 10 9 8 7 6 5 4 3 2 1   13 14 15 16 17 18/0

Printed in the U.S.A.   40

First edition, October 2013

❧ *Contents* ❧

❧ *Chapter 1* ❧

𝒲ho were the Pilgrims?

On September 6, 1620, a ship called the *Mayflower* set sail from England with 102 passengers. These people became known as the **Pilgrims.** A pilgrim is someone who makes a long journey. These Pilgrims left their homes in Europe to find a better life in America.

It took the *Mayflower* nine weeks to cross the Atlantic Ocean. The Pilgrims planned to settle in what is now New York. But their ship was blown off course in stormy weather. The Pilgrims landed in Cape Cod on the **coast** of Massachusetts. Eventually, they settled in an empty **Indian** village near Plymouth, across the bay from where they first landed.

TRUTH or MYTH?

The Pilgrims were the first people from England
to settle in Massachusetts.

MYTH! In 1602, English traders built a fort on the island of Cuttyhunk.
But life was too hard, so they left.

Why did the Pilgrims leave England?

All English people were supposed to belong to the same
church. But the Pilgrims didn't agree with the ideas of the
Church of England. They wanted their own church, so they
left England.

For twelve years, the Pilgrims lived in Holland. They had
freedom to pray to God as they liked. But they had to work
long hours, six days a week, for little money. Their children
forgot their English ways. Many spoke only Dutch. It was
time for the Pilgrims to find a new home.

HOE GAAT HET MET U?

ER... OKAY.

How did the Pilgrims pay for their trip to America?

To get to America, the Pilgrims made a *bad* business deal with an English trading company. The trading company gave the Pilgrims money to buy ships and supplies. In exchange, the Pilgrims agreed to send back **beaver furs** and wood **timber** from the New World. They promised to do this for *seven years*! After that, the Pilgrims could work for themselves.

They bought two ships for the voyage. The Pilgrims left Holland on the *Speedwell*. It leaked badly, so they gave up on that ship. A bigger ship was waiting for them in England. The Pilgrims from Holland tried to board the *Mayflower*. All but twenty Pilgrims could fit into the crowded ship.

On September 6, 1620, the *Mayflower* set sail from Plymouth, England.

Who made the trip across the Atlantic?

A lot of people. There were 102 passengers and 2 dogs, a spaniel and a mastiff. Twenty-five sailors, led by Master Christopher Jones, made up the crew of the *Mayflower*.

> ### *Passengers*
> 69 adults
> 14 teenagers
> 19 children
> 2 dogs
> 25 crew members

What jobs did the Pilgrims have at home?

The Pilgrims were shopkeepers, weavers, tailors, shoemakers, carpenters, blacksmiths, and farmers. No one had experience in setting up a new **colony** in the wilderness.

Some outsiders joined the Pilgrims for the adventure. They hoped to become rich in the New World. But everyone was afraid of meeting up with unfriendly Indians.

CHECK YOUR PILGRIM IQ

The passengers on the *Mayflower* came to the New World to

a) worship in their own way.

b) get rich.

c) escape poverty.

d) have an adventure.

The answer is *all of the above*. The Pilgrims were made up of different kinds of people. About half came for religious reasons. Some came because they needed jobs. Others wanted to **trade** with the Indians and make money. All came to find a better life.

Who's Who on board the *Mayflower*?

MILES STANDISH

WILLIAM BRADFORD

CAPTAIN MILES STANDISH

Miles Standish joined the Pilgrims in Holland. He was a trained soldier, so the Pilgrims put Miles in charge of the guns on the *Mayflower*. He was a small man, but strong. Miles had red hair and a bad temper. The settlers respected his military skills and followed his orders.

WILLIAM BRADFORD

William Bradford was thirty-one years old when he set sail on the *Mayflower*. He knew the Bible by heart and had taught himself to read and write.

William was elected governor. He was a wise leader and kept the peace with the Indians for thirty-three years. We know about the early years of the colony from his book *History of Plymouth Plantation*.

PRISCILLA MULLINS AND JOHN ALDEN

Both Priscilla and John came over on the *Mayflower*. Priscilla was seventeen when her parents died that first winter. John was twenty-one and an important leader. They became famous in the poem by Henry Wadsworth Longfellow called "The Courtship of Miles Standish."

TRUTH or MYTH?

Priscilla married John Alden.

TRUTH! The story was told by generations of Aldens before Longfellow wrote his poem. John's best friend was Miles Standish. As the story goes, Captain Standish liked Priscilla but was shy, so he asked John to propose marriage to Priscilla for *him*. But Priscilla was sweet on John instead. She asked John to speak for himself!

Who was the youngest Pilgrim?

As the *Mayflower* sailed the Atlantic, a baby boy was born. The baby's father, Stephen Hopkins, named this newest Pilgrim *Oceanus*!

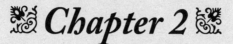

Chapter 2

How did the Pilgrims get to America?

By sea. The Pilgrims had planned to take two ships across the dangerous Atlantic. But the *Speedwell* leaked and had to be left behind. It was small, at 50 feet long. Luckily, the *Mayflower*, a bigger ship about 100 feet long, was able to make the voyage.

TRUTH or MYTH?

The *Mayflower* was a passenger ship.

MYTH! The *Mayflower* was built to carry cargo, not people. For eleven years, the *Mayflower* had sailed across the English Channel transporting French wine to London.

THE

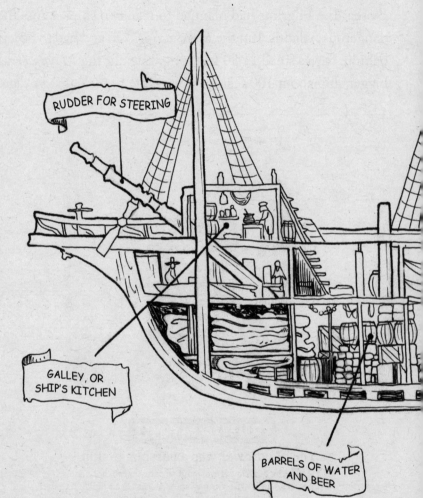

RUDDER FOR STEERING

GALLEY, OR
SHIP'S KITCHEN

BARRELS OF WATER
AND BEER

MAYFLOWER

CAPTAIN'S CABIN

DECK FOR SAILORS

FOOD SUPPLIES
AND CARGO

PASSENGERS AREA BELOW MAIN DECK

Did the Pilgrims sail the ship themselves?

No. They hired a crew. Christopher Jones was part owner and master of the *Mayflower*. John Clark was the **pilot** who steered the ship. The year before, he had sailed to Jamestown, an English colony in Virginia. The ship's **surgeon** was Giles Heale. Young John Alden was the **cooper**.

IS A COOPER LIKE A COP?

NO, THE COOPER CHECKS THE BARRELS OF WATER FOR LEAKS!

Jamestown, 1607

Thirteen years before the Pilgrims sailed to the New World, 105 Englishmen had settled in Virginia. Their leader was Captain John Smith. The Virginia settlers grew tobacco and sold it in England for profit.

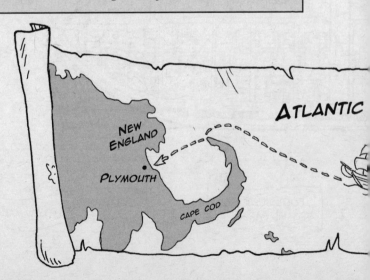

ATLANTIC

NEW ENGLAND

PLYMOUTH

CAPE COD

How did the Pilgrims find their way across the Atlantic?

Master Jones had a **compass** and other navigating tools. He used maps and charts from earlier explorers. The map made by Captain John Smith in 1614 showed the coastline from Virginia to Maine.

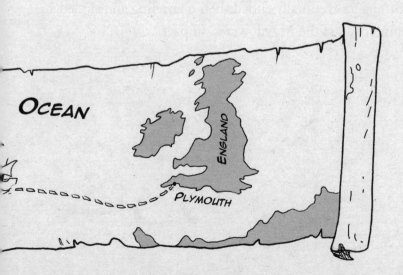

Pocahontas saved John Smith's life and later married him.

MYTH! There's no proof that Pocahontas begged her father, the Indian chief Powhatan, to let John live. She certainly didn't marry him. Pocahontas was only ten, and he was an old man!

Did the people on board the *Mayflower* get along?

Not always. All the passengers today are known as Pilgrims. But at the time, the Pilgrims divided themselves into two groups. About forty were Separatists, who had left the Church of England for religious reasons. The other sixty called themselves Strangers. Most of the Strangers had joined the ship in England. They wanted to get rich in the New World.

The Strangers felt like outsiders. They were suspicious of the church people and argued with them a lot. The Pilgrims and Strangers eventually ended their quarreling and signed an agreement called the Mayflower Compact.

One of the first written laws in America was called

a) the Declaration of Independence.

b) the Bill of Rights.

c) the Mayflower Compact.

d) the Constitution.

The answer is c. The Mayflower Compact gave the Pilgrims fair rules that all promised to follow. The people voted on many issues and elected a governor. Decisions were made by **"majority rule."**

TRUTH or MYTH?

Everyone on the *Mayflower* signed the new agreement.

MYTH! Forty-one Pilgrim men signed (some were too sick!). Women couldn't sign. They weren't allowed the same rights.

Did the hired sailors like the Pilgrims?

No. The sailors laughed at the Pilgrims' church songs. They made fun when the passengers got seasick. The Pilgrims didn't like the sailors, either. The sailors used bad language and mocked the Pilgrims' prayers.

❧ *Chapter 3* ❧
Was it easy to cross the Atlantic on the *Mayflower*?

No. It was a long and dangerous voyage. The *Mayflower* was a small ship in a big ocean. Day after day, for nine weeks, the little ship battled high winds and rough seas. One time, the *Mayflower* almost sank. The main beam had cracked. The crew used a giant iron screw to fix the beam that held the deck.

During a bad storm, Master Jones ordered passengers to stay below, but young John Howland sneaked on deck. A giant wave tossed him overboard. On the next wave, John came to the surface. The sailors tossed a boat hook. It caught on John's leather jacket. The crew pulled John to safety.

What was it like on board the *Mayflower*?

Crowded. The Pilgrims started with two ships, but only the *Mayflower* made the crossing. Twenty-five sailors along with 102 Pilgrims, two dogs, their belongings, and their supplies were stuffed into one ship!

Each family was allowed one trunk. The family Bible had its own box. Women brought pots and pans for cooking. Men brought guns and tools. There was no room for toys.

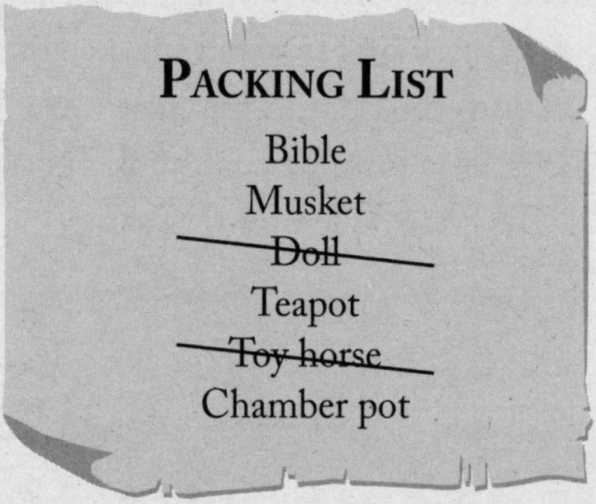

PACKING LIST

Bible
Musket
~~Doll~~
Teapot
~~Toy horse~~
Chamber pot

Where did the passengers stay most of the time?

Below deck. Master Jones allowed twenty Pilgrim leaders to move into his cabin. The rest crammed below deck. It was cold and damp. There was little light and no place to wash. The Pilgrims wore the same clothes every day. With so many people in such a tight space, the air smelled bad.

What did the Pilgrims eat and drink on board ship?

Usually a meal of pickled beef, moldy cheese, and biscuits called **hardtack**. After long weeks at sea, the food became full of worms and bugs. The water and beer started to taste sour. A lot of passengers got sick. One of them died.

TRUTH or MYTH?

Even kids drank beer.

TRUTH! The water in the barrels had turned bad. It was safer for everyone to drink beer.

What did the Pilgrims do all day on the *Mayflower*?

The Pilgrims were religious people. Every morning and evening, they knelt and prayed. They listened to Bible readings and prayed for a safe passage. The Pilgrims often sang church songs, called **psalms.**

The kids on board liked to run around the deck and climb the ship's riggings. They peered over the railing to look for whales and dolphins. When the seas got rough, the kids had to stay below deck.

TRUTH or MYTH?

The Pilgrims had only Bibles to read.
MYTH! William Brewster, a Pilgrim leader, had brought along his library of books.

Where did people sleep on board?

The crew slept apart from the passengers. Some sailors had **hammocks.** But most sailors slept on the floor of the top deck.

Most of the Pilgrims slept on the floor below the main deck. About twenty pe ople fit tightly into a small boat, called a **shallop**, which the Pilgrims brought with them. Later, the boat would carry men to explore the shore.

What about toilets?

There weren't any bathrooms on board. The Pilgrims used chamber pots. Servants emptied the pots into the ocean every day.

When did the Pilgrims reach the New World?

The Pilgrims saw land on November 9, 1620, after nine long weeks at sea. Master Jones believed it was the bay side coast of Cape Cod. Behind the cliffs of sand were hills covered with trees. For hours, they stared at the dangerous low rocks and breaking waves. A wind carried the *Mayflower* along the coast until the Pilgrims found a sandy beach. They dropped **anchor.**

Why did they need to get off the *Mayflower*?

The Pilgrims had been at sea for sixty-five days. Many of the passengers were sick. Only a little food was left, and most of it was rotten. The Pilgrims needed fresh water. Everyone wanted to set foot on land again. But they had to stay on the ship until they found a safe place to land.

TRUTH or MYTH?

The Pilgrims saw Indians right away.

TRUTH! Captain Standish took sixteen men and rowed a longboat to explore the shore. They marched along the beach. Suddenly, they saw native people ahead. The Indians ran away and hid. For miles, the Pilgrims followed their footprints to an empty Indian village. They found a basket of corn, but no Indians. The Pilgrims took the corn to use later as seed to plant their own corn.

Who else got off the ship?

On Monday morning, the women grabbed dirty clothes and went ashore to do the washing in fresh water. At last, the kids were free to run around. Some sailors ate **mussels** and clams they found along the shore. Many got sick from eating the shellfish on empty stomachs!

Did the Pilgrims find a place to live?

Not right away. The water around the Cape was shallow. The Pilgrims needed a deeper harbor closer to land. They explored the coast of Cape Cod for a good place to live. November was already past. It got colder every day. There was barely enough time to build houses before winter set in.

Master Jones checked his charts. The ship's pilot pointed to Plymouth on John Smith's map. It was across the bay. A group of men got into the shallop. Overnight, winds carried the small boat across the bay toward the shore.

What did the Pilgrims find at Plymouth?

Four men from the shallop went ashore at dawn. They didn't see any Indians. The hilltop above the harbor was a good place for a fort. They could build houses on the side of the hill. A brook of fresh water was nearby. To the south, they found old Indian cornfields. The land was empty and ready to farm.

TRUTH or MYTH?

The Pilgrims stepped on Plymouth Rock when they came to shore.

Probably **TRUTH!** There was a big rock at the harbor where the shallop pulled in. Today, a famous rock marks the landing site. Most people believe the **legend** of Plymouth Rock, but we can't say for certain that it is true.

Chapter 4

How did the Pilgrims survive in the new land?

It was mid-December when the Pilgrims dropped anchor in Plymouth. They used the shallop to move back and forth from ship to shore. Some Pilgrims stayed on board the *Mayflower*, while others set up camp and worked on land.

Their first job was to build a village. The winter was bitter cold, and wet. About twenty men stayed at camp at one time. The men cut timber for houses. It was hard work, and the bad weather slowed them down.

How did the Pilgrims celebrate Christmas?

On December 25, 1620, they worked all day as usual. The Pilgrims did not believe in celebrating Christmas. There were no Christmas trees or exchange of gifts. The Pilgrims built their first house on December 25. At night, the tired Pilgrims returned to the ship. On the *Mayflower*, the sailors celebrated by eating, drinking, and singing holiday carols.

Did all the Pilgrims survive that first winter?

No. About half became ill and died. Of the 102 Pilgrims, only 52 were alive by spring. They had little food and no fresh fruit. Some got **scurvy**, a disease of the gums, so their teeth fell out. Many had fevers and bad coughs. They died from lung infections.

The Pilgrims buried their dead at night. They didn't want the Indians to know they were so weak. The Pilgrims were afraid of an Indian attack.

The Pilgrims built a large common house. It was used to shelter workers during storms and to store tools and guns. Later, the common house was filled with beds for the sick and dying.

What was the plan of the village?

The Pilgrims built houses along one main street, from the harbor to the top of the hill. Plots for nineteen families were marked out. Not everyone had a house. Small families lived with big families. Unmarried men crowded in with families. The Pilgrims drew lots to decide who got the houses. Governor Bradford had the biggest house.

B IS FOR BRADFORD!

TRUTH or MYTH?

The Pilgrims built log cabins.

MYTH! The Pilgrims had never seen a log cabin! They built houses like the ones they had in England. They split tree trunks to make posts to frame the walls. Branches were woven in between the posts. Clay was stuffed into the empty spaces. The roofs were covered with **thatch** made of bundles of grass from the river. There was no glass, so windows were tiny and covered with paper to let in light.

What were the Pilgrim houses like inside?

Seven houses were built the first year. They were small with only one room. Space was tight. There was a loft for sleeping and storage. A huge fireplace with a stone chimney filled the back wall. The fireplace was so big that a man could stand up inside!

Did the Pilgrims have furniture?

Some Pilgrim leaders brought chairs, chests, and beds. Wood planks were laid on barrels to make simple tables and benches. After eating, they were taken apart and placed against the wall until the next meal.

Did the Pilgrims expect an Indian attack?

Yes. The Pilgrims knew the Indians were watching them. They heard them in the woods. They found the Indians' corn and animal traps. The Indians were out there, but they were hiding.

On the top of the hill, Captain Standish had built a platform for the cannons. The guns protected the harbor below. To the west were pine-covered hills. The Pilgrims could see smoke from Indian fires rising among the trees.

TRUTH or MYTH?

The Indians were afraid of the Pilgrims.

TRUTH! The Indians had reason to stay away from the Pilgrims. Four years before, a great sickness had killed all the Indians who lived in Plymouth. This disease was possibly **smallpox**. It was brought to New England by the European fishermen and traders who traveled along the coast. People like the Pilgrims!

Who had settled in Plymouth before the Pilgrims?

The Patuxet Indians had lived in Plymouth for many years. They came each spring to plant corn, fish, and hunt. This was their summer camp. In winter, the Patuxets moved inland to their home in the forest.

The Patuxet tribe was part of the Wampanoag (Wam-pa-NO-ag) nation. Many tribes made up the Wampanoag, or "people of the dawn." These native people had lived in the New England area for thousands of years. Their great leader was Chief Massasoit (Mas-uh-SOH-it).

Did the Pilgrims have to clear the land for farming?

No. The Patuxets had already removed trees and rocks from Plymouth land. They had planted many acres of corn to feed the tribe over the winter. The Pilgrims had found the Indians' old cornfields. All they had to do was pull up weeds and plant new seeds.

Did Chief Massasoit attack the Pilgrims?

No. He watched and waited all winter long. He sent his warriors to spy on the Pilgrims. They told him that the Pilgrims didn't have much food. Massasoit even knew about the dead people the Pilgrims had buried in secret.

The chief saw that the Pilgrims were different from earlier explorers. They had brought their women and children with them. They kept to themselves and built houses. It was clear that the Pilgrims were planning to stay for a long time.

⚜️ *Chapter 5* ⚜️

𝒲hen did the Pilgrims finally see Indians?

In the spring. The Pilgrims were slowly coming out of that terrible winter. The sick who had survived were rising from their sickbeds. The men were getting stronger. Women and children were planting gardens. Plymouth Colony was coming to life.

The Pilgrims went out hunting for fresh meat. They hid behind bushes and watched Indians walk by. They saw more in the woods. One day, Captain Standish and his men left some tools in the forest. They returned and found that their axes were gone.

Who made the first move?

Massasoit did. It was time to meet the Pilgrims. Chief Massasoit sent a warrior to Plymouth village. On March 16, 1621 a tall Indian named Samoset walked quietly down the main street. He was wearing only a breechcloth.

What happened when the Pilgrims saw Samoset?

The Pilgrims stopped what they were doing. They stared at the nearly naked man. Miles Standish quickly grabbed his **musket** and rushed out of the common house. Samoset slowly raised his hands. He called out a greeting: "Welcome, English!"

The men put down their guns. They were surprised and relieved to hear their own language. This was a friendly Indian.

What was Samoset's next word?

"Beer." Samoset asked for something to drink. Then he told the Pilgrims he was sent by Chief Massasoit. He explained that their village was on Patuxet land, and every Indian in the tribe had died from a disease.

Samoset carried greetings to the Pilgrims from Chief Massasoit, the great leader of the region. He told them Massasoit lived at Pokanoket, about forty miles to the southwest, near Narragansett Bay. He explained that the Nauset tribe lived in the part of the Cape where the Pilgrims had stolen the corn!

- WAMPANOAG TERRITORY, 1620 -

PATUXET (PLYMOUTH COLONY)

CAPE COD BAY

NAUSET

POKANOKUT

NARRAGANSETT BAY

TRUTH or MYTH?

Samoset was a Wampanoag Indian.

MYTH! Samoset came from an Abenaki tribe in Maine. He had learned some English from Europeans who fished up and down the coast.

Did Samoset stay with the Pilgrims long?

No. Samoset wanted to stay overnight, but the Pilgrims didn't trust him. They planned to take him to the *Mayflower*. They got into the shallop together, but the winds were too strong. Finally, Stephen Hopkins and his family took Samoset to their home. They watched him closely all night long.

Samoset left the next morning. He returned to Massasoit's village with gifts from the Pilgrims. The Pilgrims had given the chief a knife, a hat, shoes, a shirt, and bracelets.

The Pilgrims gave Massasoit gifts, but they *didn't* give him

a) clothes.

b) guns.

c) jewelry.

d) tools.

The answer is *b*. The Indians had bows and arrows. Only the Pilgrims had muskets. The Pilgrims wanted to keep an advantage in an attack.

Did Samoset make the Pilgrims a promise?

Yes. Samoset said he would return in a few days. He would bring some of Massasoit's men with him. Samoset's English was poor. The Pilgrims weren't sure of all he told them.

Who came with Samoset on his next visits?

Two days later, Samoset returned with some of Massasoit's men. The Indians left their bows and arrows outside of the village. They had beaver furs that Samoset hoped to trade with the Pilgrims. A few days later, Samoset came again. He brought four other Indians. Squanto was one of them.

Who was Squanto?

Squanto was a Patuxet Indian, but he had been away for six years. An English explorer had captured Squanto in 1614 and taken him to Europe as a slave. Squanto escaped to London and learned English. He returned to America as a **translator** on an English trading ship. Squanto spoke nearly perfect English.

When Squanto's ship stopped at Patuxet, Squanto saw that his village had been wiped out by **plague**, a terrible disease. The Pilgrims were the new inhabitants of Plymouth. Squanto went to Massasoit and convinced the chief to make friends with the Pilgrims. He knew that the English guns could protect the Wampanoags from their enemy, the Narragansett Indians.

How did Squanto bring peace to Plymouth?

Squanto played an important role in bringing the Pilgrims and the Wampanoags together. He spoke both languages. He understood the ways of both peoples. Squanto helped to negotiate a **treaty** between the Pilgrims and the Indians. They shared a pipe of tobacco and drank "strong water." The treaty was signed. There was peace in Plymouth for more than fifty years.

MASSASOIT AND THE PILGRIMS AGREED:

Not to attack each other.

To return all stolen goods.

To fight off each other's enemies.

To leave weapons at home when visiting.

TRUTH or MYTH?

Massasoit was shaking from fear at the meeting.
TRUTH! But Massasoit wasn't afraid of the Pilgrims' guns. Squanto had told Massasoit that the Pilgrims kept the plague in barrels buried under the common house!

Did the *Mayflower* stay at Plymouth?

No. On April 5, 1621, the *Mayflower* set sail for England. Some sailors had been ill. A few died over the winter. But the crew was mostly healthy now. The Pilgrims filled the ship with timber and fish to bring to their business partners in England.

Not one Pilgrim returned. All those who had survived the hard times wanted to stay in the New World.

🐉 *Chapter 6* 🐉

𝒲hat did Squanto teach the Pilgrims?

Squanto taught them survival skills. The Pilgrims had left their homes in Europe. Now, they were living in the New England wilderness. Over the bitter winter, half the Pilgrims had died. They were in trouble.

Squanto took the Pilgrims into the forest. He showed them native plants and wild berries. Most were good to eat, but some were poisonous. Squanto pointed to special plants that could be used as medicine. He showed them the Indian way to fish, hunt, and plant corn. With Squanto's help, the Pilgrims were able to feed themselves and get healthy again.

What did the Pilgrims eat to celebrate the peace treaty?

Freshwater eels! Squanto took the Pilgrims to the river. The Pilgrims watched as Squanto stamped his feet along the riverbank. After a while, eels wiggled out of the shallow water and rose to the surface.

At this time of year, the eels were lying asleep in the mud. Squanto caught the eels with his hands. They made a fine dinner. The Pilgrims praised the eels as "fat and sweet."

TRUTH or MYTH?

The Pilgrims ate all the fish they caught.

MYTH! The Pilgrims preserved most of the fish to eat later. They hung the fish on long poles and dried them in the sunshine. Then, the Pilgrims salted the fish and stored them in barrels.

Did the Pilgrims eat a lot of shellfish?

No. Most of the Pilgrims didn't like **quahogs** (KO-hogs) and mussels. Too bad, since there were a lot on the shore. The Pilgrims mostly fed the shellfish to their pigs.

INDIAN CLAMBAKE

On special days, the Wampanoags dug a big hole in the sand. Stones were heated in a bonfire. The hot stones were put into the pit and covered with wet **rockweed** gathered along the shore. The squishy seaweed popped in the heat of the fire.

On top, the Indians piled layers of clams and fish and more rockweed. They added native corn for the last layer. Finally, the pit was covered with more rockweed.

Hours later, when the steam had cooked everything, the Indians raked open the pit and ate the food.

Did the Pilgrims have seeds for planting?

Yes. They brought barley, pea, and wheat seeds with them. But these plants grew well in England, not in the rocky soil of New England.

I GIVE UP!!

Where did they get corn seeds?

The Pilgrims stole corn from the Nauset Indians when they explored the coast of Cape Cod. They followed Indian footprints to an abandoned Indian camp. The Pilgrims found mounds of dirt. When they dug, they pulled out two baskets of Indian corn that the Indians had left behind. The Pilgrims were lucky. They would be able to plant the corn in the spring.

TRUTH or MYTH?

Squanto showed the Pilgrims how to plant corn.

TRUTH! Squanto knew the soil was poor. The corn wouldn't grow in the old Indian cornfields without **fertilizer**.

Squanto taught the Pilgrims how to make rows of small mounds about three feet wide. Then, the Pilgrims dug a hole in each mound and put in three dead fish! The hole was covered with dirt. The fish decayed. Two weeks later, the Pilgrims dropped four kernels of corn in the same hole and covered it again.

The fish worked as fertilizer to help the corn grow strong and tall. Twenty acres of corn were planted this way.

Later, beans and squash were added to the mounds. The vines wrapped around the growing cornstalks as they grew. These plants shaded the corn from the hot sun and stopped weeds from growing.

Did the Pilgrims hunt and fish for food?

Yes. The woods around Plymouth were filled with game and wild birds. The Indians showed the Pilgrims how to fish for trout in the streams. They used bone for hooks and lobster meat for bait.

Squanto knew that the rivers filled with herring each spring. Thousands of the silver-backed fish raced up the river to lay their eggs. Squanto taught the Pilgrims how to catch these fish in the shallow waters. They would need lots of fish for planting corn.

But the wild turkeys of New England were bigger and faster. The Pilgrims learned to track their footprints in the woods. Wild turkeys made a good meal.

What else did the Pilgrims hunt?

Squanto taught the Pilgrims how to track small animals and build traps. He showed them the best places to hunt deer, turkey, and waterbirds.

Who got caught in a deer trap?

William Bradford! The governor-to-be was with Miles Standish and some men, exploring the coast. They followed a deer path. One of the men pointed to a bent sapling. Hidden were a cord with a noose and a bait of acorns. Bradford took a step closer and the tree branch jerked upright. He found himself hanging by one leg, upside down!

What was Plymouth's most valuable export to England?

Beaver furs. Squanto helped Miles Standish trade with the Indians for beaver furs. The furs were sent back to England. They were used to make felt hats, which were popular at the time.

STEPS TO BUILD A BEAVER SNARE:

✔ Look for beaver signs: paw prints on a riverbank, tree stumps chewed to a point, dams built from logs.

✔ Find a two-foot-wide funnel, or narrow space, on the game trail.

✔ Look for an anchor nearby for your **snare**, such as a tree trunk.

✔ Tie a knot on one end of the snare. Make a five-inch noose, wide enough for the beaver to slip its head through.

✔ Tie the other end of the cord to the anchor.

✔ Hang the noose in the middle of the trail, about two inches off the ground.

✔ Use sticks to prop your noose open in the shape of a circle.

🐉 *Chapter 7* 🐉

𝒲ho did the work around Plymouth village?

Everyone worked. There was a lot to do to settle the colony and survive in the wilderness. In the spring, corn was planted. All the men worked the fields. They fished, set traps, and hunted in the woods.

The women planted small gardens. They took care of the chickens and farm animals that they had brought on the *Mayflower*. It was a big job to make meals from the little food they had.

The children had chores, too. They gathered wood and carried water. Pigs roamed in the street. When the tide was low, the children herded the pigs down to the seashore to feed on the shellfish.

What foods did the Pilgrims eat?

There was plenty of fresh meat. Rabbits, squirrels, and deer made great stews. The Pilgrims had fish and lobsters. There were wild turkeys, ducks, and geese. Once in a while, they boiled a chicken.

The Pilgrims had fresh berries and vegetables, such as squash and pumpkin. **Herbs** from the gardens added flavor. The food in Plymouth was better than in England, and there were more types of food!

TRUTH or MYTH?

The Pilgrims got their milk from cows.

MYTH! The Pilgrims didn't have any cows. But they had brought goats with them. They drank goats' milk and made cheese and butter.

Who drank beer?

Everyone did. The water in European cities wasn't safe to drink. It made people sick. Beer was safer to drink. Children drank it, too.

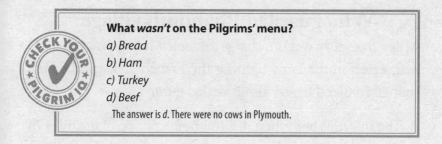
Did the Pilgrims have fresh bread?

Yes. The women baked bread in a community oven, about twenty loaves at one time. They made "one-third bread" of equal parts of wheat, rye, and Indian corn flour. There were no mills in Plymouth. The Pilgrims had to grind the flour by hand.

Who guarded Plymouth village?

Miles Standish was in charge of defending Plymouth. He had served in the army fighting the French and was the only trained soldier. He was also a skilled gunner.

The Pilgrims built their meetinghouse on top of the hill. On its upper deck, they placed six cannons in a ring. The Indians weren't the only potential enemy. The gun deck protected the harbor below. The Pilgrims were always watching for French and Spanish ships, enemies of the English. Even pirate ships were a danger!

Did the Pilgrims have any experience with firearms?

Miles Standish trained the men to be guards and soldiers. They learned how to "exercise their arms." He taught all men in town how to load and shoot muskets. They were drilled daily. The men marched in formation and fired their guns on command.

The Pilgrims guarded the guns 24/7. Each man had to take a turn on sentry duty.

What rules did everyone have to obey?

The Pilgrims elected leaders and set up rules that everyone agreed to follow. All Pilgrims had to work six days a week. The days were long, and the work was hard. Pilgrims got up at the crack of dawn and went to bed right after supper. Everyone had to attend church on Sunday.

It was a crime to get drunk. There was no stealing. No one could curse or use bad language.

When someone broke the rules, the governor made the final decision. If guilty, the governor's assistant carried out the punishment.

Everyone followed orders and did guard duty.

MYTH! John Billington was a troublemaker. One day, he refused to obey orders from Captain Standish and used bad language. As punishment, he was sentenced to have his neck and feet tied together and to be tossed in the street.

There were no jails. Pilgrims who broke the law were punished in public. Everyone saw their shame. Children who disobeyed their parents could be put in stocks, just like adults.

How is a person "set in stocks"?

He or she sits on a bench, with his wrists and ankles inserted through a wooden board. The person could stay this way out in public for days.

Did the Pilgrims go to church?

Yes and no. They spent Sundays in prayer. But they hadn't built a church. Services were held at the meetinghouse at the top of the hill. The Pilgrims sat directly below the fort's gun deck. Because gunpowder was stored there, the Pilgrims couldn't light a fire.

The Pilgrims prayed and sang psalms from 8:00 a.m. to noon, and again from 2:00 to 6:00 p.m. They didn't have a minister. William Brewster led the service and gave the sermon.

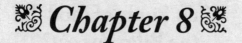 Chapter 8

What did Pilgrim children do all day?

They worked hard. Every Pilgrim had a job to do, even the youngest ones. Pilgrim children had plenty of chores. They gathered wood and carried fresh water from the brook. Chickens had to be fed and eggs collected. Gardens needed weeding. Girls helped with cooking and cleaning. Boys watched the fields and threw stones to keep birds and wolves away from the corn.

Children gathered berries in the woods. They dug for clams and picked mussels off the rocks on shore. They caught eels and cut reeds for the thatch roofs.

What kinds of food did the Pilgrims eat?

They ate a lot of fish, deer, and wild birds. Corn was always on the menu. Corn cobs were hung out to dry. Women pounded the kernels by hand to make flour. Pilgrims used the corn flour to make a thick porridge or to bake bread.

Pumpkins were an important part of the Pilgrim diet. The Pilgrims enjoyed stewed pumpkins all winter long.

YUCK! PUMPKIN STEW AGAIN!!

Did they eat a lot of English foods?

The Pilgrims brought seeds with them from England. The wheat and barley seeds didn't grow well in the hot New England sun. Onions, carrots, and some herbs did better in the small gardens.

Did the children eat with the rest of the family?

No. The main meal was served at noon. Children and servants served the meal. Adults ate first. Children ate the food that was left over. They ate standing up. Mealtimes were messy. Everyone ate with their fingers. Sometimes they used knives. A few people had wooden spoons.

What foods were missing during that first year?

The Pilgrims had no apples, potatoes, or honey. They ran out of the sugar they had brought with them. Later, the Pilgrims learned how to tap maple trees to get sap. They made syrup from the sap to sweeten wild berries and pumpkin stew.

Did Pilgrim children go to school?

No. There was no schoolhouse. Not everyone could read. Some fathers gave lessons by reading from the Bible. Children probably practiced their ABC's on pieces of wood.

Women weren't taught to read or write. The Pilgrims believed a young girl would "destroy her brain" by reading, since she was not as strong as a man!

Until they were six, boys and girls wore dresses and white caps. By the age of seven, they dressed like adult men and women and shared in the work of the village.

Where did the Pilgrims sleep?

Pilgrim houses had tight sleeping spaces. Adult beds were made of rope webbing. The mattresses were big sacks, filled with rags or feathers.

Babies had cradles. Younger children pulled out a **trundle bed** from under their parents' bed. Older children climbed a ladder and slept in the loft.

The Pilgrims used rugs for bed covers. Everyone went to sleep around seven or eight o'clock.

The Pilgrims had only the clothes they brought with them. They washed clothes twice a year. They smelled pretty bad.

What kinds of medicines did the Pilgrims have?

Like many people of their time, the Pilgrims used plants and herbs to cure everyday aches. They made a paste of animal fat and wild daisies to put on cuts and open sores. The leaves and fruit of wild roses were used to make a tea for coughs and colds.

Samuel Fuller was the settlement's surgeon. Sometimes he tried to cure sick Pilgrims by bleeding them. He made cuts in their arms so that the "bad" blood could flow out. This usually made the patients worse!

Did any Pilgrim kids get into trouble?

The teenage Billington boys were always pulling pranks. While the *Mayflower* was anchored off Cape Cod, Francis Billington played with muskets on board. The guns were kept near barrels of gunpowder. Sparks from a gun started a fire. Francis almost blew up the ship!

Francis's brother, John Junior, was no better. One day, Junior disappeared. His mother thought her son had been kidnapped by Indians! Miles Standish and Squanto hunted down the boy. They found John Junior living with the Nauset Indians. He was wearing beads and feathers and having a great time.

❧ *Chapter 9* ❧

*W*hy did the Pilgrims celebrate Thanksgiving?

The Pilgrims had a lot to be thankful for. They had survived a dangerous sea voyage and built a village in the wilderness. No Indians had attacked. At the end of their first dreadful winter, fifty Pilgrims were still alive.

It was a good summer. There was plenty of food. In England, the Pilgrims had always celebrated the harvest. So they decided to have a big feast in Plymouth, too.

The hunters set out into the forest. The ponds were filled with migrating ducks and geese. Turkeys roamed the woods. After a day of shooting, the men returned with lots of wild birds.

Who cooked and prepared the food?

The women and children did most of the cooking. There were corncobs to grind, birds to pluck, and vegetables to pick. The women baked corn bread and puddings. Stewed eels, boiled lobsters, and clam stews cooked slowly over the fires. Smells of roasting geese and turkeys filled the air.

How did the Pilgrims cook the turkeys?

Turkeys were cooked in fireplaces. A thin iron rod called a *spit* was pushed through the bird. The rod was set close to the flame. The rod had a handle on one end. It was a child's job to turn the handle. Sometimes it took all day for the turkey to cook.

What else was served at the first Thanksgiving?

The Pilgrims cooked codfish and sea bass. There was rabbit stew and vegetables, such as beets and squash. They munched on walnuts and chestnuts during the meal.

CHECK YOUR ✓ PILGRIM IQ

Which of these foods were *not* served at the first Thanksgiving?

a) Roast turkey and venison

b) Stewed eels and lobster

c) Pumpkin pie and cranberry sauce

d) Corn bread and puddings

The answer is *c*. The Pilgrims had pumpkins and cranberries. But they didn't have wheat or sugar to make pumpkin pie and cranberry sauce.

Was there anything special to drink at the feast?

The Pilgrims made new beer from the barley they had planted. They didn't know about tea or coffee. It would be fifty years before traders from China and Africa brought these drinks to England and later to America.

Who did the Pilgrims invite to celebrate with them?

On the day of the celebration, Chief Massasoit showed up. But he didn't come alone. He brought ninety extra guests! Governor Bradford happily invited the Wampanoags to join the feast.

The Pilgrims didn't expect to feed so many people. Massasoit sent out his hunters. The warriors came back with five deer. In no time, there was plenty of meat ready to barbecue.

The Pilgrims rolled out barrels and placed wooden planks on top. These tables were set up both indoors and outdoors. Massasoit and his chiefs sat with Governor Bradford and the Pilgrim leaders at the "high table." There weren't enough tables, so some people sat on the ground.

All the dishes of food were placed on the table at once. Kids ate last. They stood on the side and waited until the adults had eaten. Then they could have their Thanksgiving dinner.

How did people eat their food?

Mostly with their hands! The Pilgrims wore big napkins, about three feet square, over their shoulders. Before people reached for food, it was the rule to wipe their fingers. The napkins were also used to hold hot meat, like turkey legs.

There weren't a lot of plates. The Pilgrims used **trenchers** instead. These were flat, square pieces of wood. The middle was hollowed out to hold food. Two people ate from one trencher.

The first Thanksgiving was one big meal.

MYTH! There was so much food that the feast lasted for three days! The Pilgrims and Indians had many meals, not just one. As long as there was food, the Indians were in no hurry to go home.

Did they spend all their time eating?

No. There was plenty of time for fun and games between meals. The Indians showed their athletic abilities. They held races and wrestling matches. Some of the Pilgrim men played stoolball, a game like cricket, and others threw weights.

Did the Pilgrims dance?

Yes. Pilgrim women danced English country dances while the men watched. The Indians entertained the Pilgrims with special tribal dances.

TRUTH or MYTH?

The Indians danced to the beat of drums.

MYTH! The Wampanoags did not have musical instruments. But they liked to sing loudly as they stomped their feet.

How did the Pilgrims entertain Massasoit and his chiefs?

Miles Standish put on a military show. He drilled his men to the beat of drums and trumpets. The Pilgrims demonstrated their shooting skills by firing their muskets.

The Indians put on their own display. They set up targets and held contests with bows and arrows.

There is no record of an official Thanksgiving Day in Plymouth until 1623. At that time, a full day was set aside by the governor for a "Thanksgiving" church service. It soon became a tradition in New England to have a special day every fall to celebrate and give thanks.

 Chapter 10

What happened in Plymouth after the first Thanksgiving?

New ships came from England. In November 1621, the *Fortune* arrived in Plymouth with thirty-five settlers. Most were men hoping to get rich in America.

Winter was coming. Now there were eighty-nine mouths to feed. The *Fortune* didn't bring any extra supplies, so Governor Bradford cut food portions in half.

In June, two other ships, the *Charity* and the *Swan*, brought sixty more men. There weren't many unmarried women in Plymouth. The men grumbled and got into trouble. By March, most of the new settlers had given up and gone home to England.

How did Plymouth colony grow?

Ships kept coming from England. Slowly, the little colony got bigger. By 1624, there were 180 people living in Plymouth.

More animals came, too. Three heifers and a bull arrived on one ship. The village also included six goats, fifty pigs, and dozens of egg-laying hens.

TRUTH or MYTH?

The Pilgrims finally paid for their trip to America on the *Mayflower*.

TRUTH! The Pilgrims owed money to their business partners in London. Over time, they sent beaver furs, wooden planks, and dried fish back to England and paid off their debt.

How did the Pilgrims solve the food problem?

Until 1623, the Pilgrims owned all the farm land together. They stored the corn in a common warehouse and shared the harvest. But there was never enough food. Governor Bradford made a decision. He divided the land, so that each man, woman, and child received one acre. Now each family could keep what it grew.

Suddenly, everyone worked much harder than before. Women and children joined the men in the fields. Each family kept the profits from selling extra corn. Free enterprise was born in America. The Pilgrims never starved again.

Who else settled in Massachusetts?

In 1630, seventeen ships carried a thousand new colonists to New England. These people, called **Puritans**, belonged to a different church. The Puritans settled to the north, in Boston. This town became the Massachusetts Bay Colony. It quickly expanded into Maine and New Hampshire and took over the region.

How do we know so much about the early Pilgrims?

The ships that came to Plymouth carried letters back and forth across the Atlantic. Some Pilgrims had left wives and children in Holland. Governor William Bradford wrote often to his London business partners.

Some Pilgrims kept journals. Governor Bradford's journal was published as the *History of Plymouth Plantation*. Edward Winslow's story of brave Pilgrims settling in the wilderness was printed in England. Longfellow's poem, "The Courtship of Miles Standish," also made the Pilgrims famous.

Who threatened the peace?

The Narragansetts, the powerful enemy of the Wampanoags, were planning to attack Plymouth colony. They sent a messenger to the Pilgrims with a bundle of arrows wrapped in rattlesnake skin. This was not a sign of friendship. Governor Bradford poured gunpowder and bullets into the snakeskin and sent it back. The Narragansetts were afraid of the Pilgrims' guns. They did not attack.

What did the Pilgrims do to protect Plymouth?

They built a twelve-foot-high wooden wall around the village. It took a month for Miles Standish and fifty men to erect this **palisade.** The gates were closed at sunset. Guards kept watch during the night.

What happened to Squanto?

With his own people dead, Squanto had adopted the Pilgrims as his family. He showed them how to plant corn. He helped Miles Standish trade with the Indians for beaver furs.

But Squanto caused some trouble, too. He tried to use his friendship with the Pilgrims to become chief of the Wampanoags. Squanto and Massasoit became enemies. But Miles Standish and Governor Bradford protected Squanto. They owed Squanto a lot. He had saved them from starving to death that difficult first year.

On a voyage to trade with Indians on Cape Cod, Squanto got sick. He died of fever with Governor Bradford at his side.

What's Plymouth like today?

Plymouth today is a modern town. The old Pilgrim village is gone. In its place is an outdoor living museum. Visitors can walk around and visit the exhibits. There is a 1627 Pilgrim settlement and a Wampanoag Indian village. A few miles away, a replica of the *Mayflower*, called the *Mayflower II*, is anchored in the harbor. Interpreters at each of these exhibits look, dress, and act like real people at that time.

The year is always 1627. Within the palisade walls, visitors can talk with Pilgrims as they carry on their daily chores. Members of today's Wampanoag tribe explain to visitors how to build canoes and cook Indian foods. On the *Mayflower II*, sailors show how to raise the sails and man the guns.

Can you visit Plymouth Rock today?

Yes. Many people come to Plymouth just to see the rock. It may or may not be the same rock that the Pilgrims stepped on when they came ashore. But the legend of Plymouth Rock has made this rock famous.

In 1741, some men building a dock uncovered a large rock on the shore. An old man pointed to the rock. His father had told him it was where the Pilgrims had landed. People from Plymouth believed him and tried to free the rock. It cracked and split when sixty oxen carted it away. The top half ended up as a monument in the town square.

Soon, people were chipping off chunks of the rock to take home as souvenirs. It was moved several times. Today, Plymouth Rock is one-third of its original size. An iron fence protects it from more than eight hundred thousand visitors a year.

When did Thanksgiving become an official holiday?

For many years, the first celebration in Plymouth was forgotten. A magazine editor in New Hampshire, Sarah Josepha Hale, read about the early Pilgrims. She worked hard to turn the tradition into a national holiday. In 1863, President Abraham Lincoln proclaimed the last Thursday of November as Thanksgiving.

Over time, everyone in the United States began celebrating Thanksgiving Day. New **immigrants** took the story of the Pilgrims to heart. Like them, the Pilgrims had left their homes to begin a new life in an unknown land.

Even the turkey has become a Thanksgiving tradition.

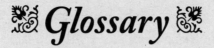 Glossary

anchor – a heavy weight attached to a boat by rope or chain. When thrown into the water, it keeps the boat in place.

beaver fur – the soft brown coat of a beaver. It was a valuable item of trade between the American colonies and seventeenth-century Europe.

chamber pot – a round container used as a toilet

coast – the land along or near an ocean or a sea

colony – land belonging to a country that is often far away from it

compass – a device with a needle pointing to magnetic north that is used to show direction

cooper – a person who makes barrels to store water, wine, or beer

draw lots – to randomly select a number or name from many tossed together in a bowl or bag

fertilizer – a chemical or natural substance added to soil to help plants grow

governor – a person elected or appointed to act as head of a group of people

hammock – a bed made by hanging a piece of cloth between two poles or trees

hardtack – a hard cracker or biscuit eaten by sailors during a long voyage

herbs – plants used as medicine or for seasoning food

immigrant – a person who comes to a country to live there

Indian – a member of the native people living in North America or South America

legend – a story from the past that people believe but that cannot be proven true

majority rule – the principle for governing a group when half the people plus at least one has the power to make decisions for the group

musket – a gun with a long barrel used by soldiers before the invention of the rifle

mussel – a shellfish with a long, dark shell

palisade – a high fence made of pointed wooden stakes used to protect a building or village

pilgrim – a person who makes a long journey, usually for religious reasons

pilot – a person who steers or guides a ship

plague – a deadly disease that spreads quickly

psalm – a song or poem from the Bible

Puritan – a member of a seventeenth-century religious group that opposed many customs of the Church of England

quahog – a type of large clam eaten as food

rockweed – a type of plant with tiny air pockets that grows in the ocean and is found on rocks along the seacoast

scurvy – a disease of bleeding gums and loose teeth caused by not eating enough fruits and vegetables with vitamin C

shallop – a small open boat with oars and a sail

smallpox – a serious disease that causes fever, a rash, and often death

snare – a trap for small animals made with a wire or rope hoop

surgeon – a doctor who performs operations by cutting into a person's body

thatch – bundles of dried grass or reeds used to make roofs of buildings

timber – trees used to produce large pieces of wood for building

trade – the business of buying or selling, or the exchange of goods between two countries or groups

translator – a person who changes words from one language into a different language, keeping the same meaning

treaty – an official agreement made between two or more countries or groups

trencher – a flat, square piece of wood with a hollowed-out center used to hold food and shared by two people

trundle bed – a sleeping platform on wheels that is stored under a bed and rolled out for use

voyage – a long journey, often by water

≈§≈

If you like *History Busters:*
The Truth (and Myths) About Thanksgiving,
you'll love discovering the facts (and myths) in

HISTORY OFFICIAL BUSTERS

THE AND MYTHS
TRUTH ∧ ABOUT
THE PRESIDENTS